The Breathing

For Gavin,

The Breathing

Mary-Ann Constantine

with much love,

Mary-Ann

Planet

Published
in Wales in 2008
by Planet

PO Box 44
Aberystwyth
Ceredigion SY23 3ZZ
Cymru/Wales

Design: Planet
Cover photo: *Cragen Cwch* © Andrew Green

Printed by Gwasg Gomer
Llandysul, Ceredigion

The publisher acknowledges the financial
support of the Welsh Books Council

ISBN: 978-0-9540881-8-7

Acknowledgements
I am grateful to *Planet* and the *New Welsh Review* where some of these stories previously appeared, and to Andrew Green for permission to use his picture on the cover. Many thanks to the Planet team for their work and encouragement.

The citations from "Lludd and Llefelys" in "The Breathing" are from the Penguin translation of *The Mabinogion* by Gwyn Jones and Thomas Jones; "The Growth of Stone" incorporates lines from Edward Owen's *Observation on the Earth, Rocks, Stones and Minerals for some Miles About Bristol*, (1754).

All characters are fictional.

For my parents

Contents

The Breathing

When the planes come over in the day his fists clench and he says bastards, and empties the rocks from the wheelbarrow to the new stone pile with an angry jolt. She, hacking back branches, would say the same if she were here. But she is lying on her back in the sunny hospital ward twenty miles away, and it is at least a minute later that she flinches at the same planes, only not quite so low, in deference to the town. Presumably when they do it for real it is the other way round — high over open country, and low, low towards the towns. Hospitals there too, but it is best not to think like that. Sun on the daffodils in her ward, and sun on the daffodils around him as he shifts the big pile of rocks so they can have a flower bed outside the kitchen window; he wants to clear it and dig it over for when she gets back. You're always shifting rocks, she said, as if it were an endearing male trait. But there were always plenty to shift.

You know how bad the noise will be from the whine that precedes them, a whine like a knife edge so sharp it is invisible, that cuts the air before the plane rips through. Thunder, then, in its wake. Some people thrill to it, and some don't mind it, and he had simply disliked it before she told him about her panic, and before they lost the child. No connection, they said at the hospital. He supposed that was right. But the farmers round here sometimes claimed they lost calves to the noise, and perhaps the panic in her blood had made the difference. At school that month he read his class of eight-year-olds the story of Lludd and Llefelys, and the three *gormesau*, the three plagues, that overcame their kingdom. And the second *gormes*, he told them, was a scream which was raised every May Eve over every hearth in the Island of Britain. *And that would pierce folk's hearts and strike them with such terror that men would lose their hue and their strength and women the fruit of their wombs, and the young men and maidens would lose their senses, and all animals and trees and the earth and the waters be left barren.* They had done him pictures, like pictures children do after war, with the animals and trees all blown over by the force of the scream. He had wanted to tell them that the planes were a kind of *gormes*, over them and over others, but their parents might not have seen it that way, and he let it go. With luck, he thought, by May Eve this year they would be well past the perilous bit. It was still only March and this time she was safe on her back in the sunny ward. This time she would not be waking in sudden terror in the middle of the day and running from the bedroom out onto the little road as the planes dived low over their house, again and again and again. Alone then, with him at work and the neighbours half a mile away, she had phoned the RAF complaints line and wept down the phone until the planes stopped coming.

He went in for a bacon sandwich and a cup of tea, and only realised when he sat down how hard he had been working. He felt shaky. The juice she liked, another novel, his marking: he piled them up on the table so he wouldn't forget, and then remembered the pussy-willow she'd asked for last time. He put his boots back on and found the secateurs where she had left them on top of the bread bin, and tramped down to the far hedge to cut a few twigs. Little soft things on the smooth stems. He felt, in a hazy half-conscious way, that he should have thought of them himself, that she shouldn't have had to ask. But there was so much to remember at the moment; it was perhaps enough to have remembered, she would be glad of that. He stopped by the stone pile on the way back to listen again. Lambs were crying, there was a far-off tractor, but he was certain now that he could hear it. What would she make of that? Back inside he washed his plate and mug and caught the end of the news on the radio, then he put everything in the car and set off.

The hospital redeemed itself. They were gentle and encouraging now, and she did relax at last, and give herself up to their care, and have faith. The first day she had been like ice with all of them, stiff with anger from the time before, with fear that it was happening again. But this time somehow the configurations of staff and equipment and time-slots fell in her favour. This time they told her what was happening, and why, and how long it would be, and what she had to do. The nurse had held her hand during the scan, and hugged her when she cried with relief. Their mismanagement the first time had amounted to cruelty. No one had said anything except *wait here for the consultant*, and the consultant, after examining her, said *come back in a week*. A long week it was, fearing the worst. At the second examination no one had said anything at all. And then, as if she was expected to know what had happened, and what would inevitably happen next: *you can put your clothes on now; you'll have to come back in a week*. And that week was the longest of all. In the end she had carried the dead child inside her for ten days and nights, mute and hopeless, and even when it came to the operation no one had explained anything, no one had said they were sorry.

As the planes came over the town her fists clenched, and she practised breathing deep and slow, dissolving the panic before it had time to gather its strength. As she breathed she watched the sun flickering on the daffodils and fell asleep, waking as he came in with his arms full of books and twigs. He sat on the end of the bed and worked his way through the exercise books, showing her the kids' pictures and reading out the good bits. They drank hospital tea, and ate his mother's biscuits, and he told her about the garden. The strangest thing happened, he said, when I was moving those stones. What was that? she asked him. As I got down the pile, he said, I thought I could hear something, a soft noise, like breathing. It took me a while to believe it, I thought it was in my head. But every time I went back with the empty wheelbarrow it got more definite. It was breathing, inside the pile. She looked amazed, delighted. What was it then? I don't know, he said. I didn't get that far down. But I imagine I'll find out soon, if it's still there when I get back.

The Fisherman
in my Bed

On the nights he was there I just picked up my things and went up to the back room, with the view of the hill instead of the sea. After the first few times I wasn't even particularly quiet. He slept deeply, he was way down, oblivious. I could open drawers for tomorrow's knickers, collect face cream from the dresser, hunt through the cupboard with my hands for a skirt, picking out the right one by feel, softly clattering the hangers. I never turned on the light, but there was enough from the landing and because he never bothered with the curtains there was sometimes the moon.

The first time was a shock of course. I may have

screamed. I know I ran outside onto the road without a torch, without my stick, and managed the several hundred yards to Elsie's, banging on the window and bursting into her front room. She was watching a game show; I did not fluster her. Is it the first already? she said, looking up at her Tropical Cruises Calendar. Already. Well there you are. And she turned the volume down imperceptibly and pointed at the other chair, getting up to make me tea. I sat and looked at the television, which was huge and poor quality. The cup and saucer trembled as she passed it over, but that was her age; that it kept trembling in my hand was an echo of my shock.

I had been there a month by then, arriving rather smugly as the last tourists left, and so more than anything it was a blow to my sense of belonging. They'd been so prompt with gifts of cake and geraniums, made efforts to find a bicycle, given me tide-tables and boat times. And it was because they had not asked about Douglas or the children that I had happily volunteered enough to fill in the obvious blanks. Then they knew enough about me, and I thought I knew enough about them, I thought the balance was about right and that the rest would come more slowly, with weeks and months, and, I hoped, years, my newness gradually rubbing away like paint. It was unfair of them not to tell me.

Elsie's explanations were expansive in style but minimal in content, assuming all kinds of knowledge I couldn't possibly have. At no point could I have stopped her to ask for basic information: Who else had them? When did it start? And there were dozens of questions that I only thought of asking later, in the days and weeks that followed. What, for example, would have happened if other, differently-minded, outsiders had bought the house? But after that evening she made it clear enough that there would be no more said. I did, at one point, try to ask why it had to be my bedroom rather than the much more convenient room at the back, but she only answered by repeating that it was the Custom, and that other people managed, and that it was only till Easter, and that I would get used to it.

And I did. At first there were days and nights of fretting about potential difficulties. The awkwardness of explaining to friends — not that I was expecting any before the spring — of explaining, my god, to the children! The never knowing when he might be there, though I tried, for the first three months, matching his appearances to numbers on the calendar, to the moon, to the wind, but they were either purely random or obeying some subtle undisclosed Island rule. Either way, they were not frequent. The unpredictability was a problem, it kept me on edge; I started sleeping in the back room, afraid he might arrive in the middle of the night and be embarrassed or offended, afraid that I would have to clamber out awkwardly in my nightie, looking my age, feeling ridiculous. But he never came at night, it was always in the afternoon, and almost always when I was out drawing or down at the Information Shack doing my distance art-classes. Once or twice I think he arrived while I was in the kitchen or the garden, letting himself in the back or front door so as not to meet me, and leaving his boots and his sou'wester, as usual, in the porch. I moved back into my room, and, by early December, had even stopped fastidiously changing all the sheets and pillowcases after a visit. I liked the smell of salt.

Gradually the only real worries I had left were to do with the possible reactions of other people, people from the outside. After the first shock and (though I say it myself) the real bravery of the first night, I was never in any fear of him physically. The third or fourth time I came home from the beach and found him sound asleep on my bed, on his back, in his overalls, in the darkening room, I stood by the door for fifteen minutes and looked at him professionally. Full lips and a dark grizzle of beard, a clear brow. A cross between an angel and a bear. As the winter moved on I sketched him in different lights and shadows, always deep asleep on his back, but with his big head tilted one way or another, his arms stretched or crooked, his face more or less shaven, the thick curly hair more or less kempt.

I went to London at Christmas, my first visit to the mainland since the move. It was a good trip, and useful — I took several paintings that would have cost a lot to send, and when I called in at the gallery spirits were high. I went to their New Year's Eve party, in spite of last year's resolutions, and listened to several people tell me how good the change had been for my work. You have such an affinity with the sea, they said. I didn't tell them, but I never paint the sea. I moved to the island to face up to it, but I never paint it. Those astonishing greens and greys, the tiny swirls and webs, are not representations of water or weed or the insides of shells, but careful reckonings of rock and lichen and the tiny plants that grow under the canopy of heather at the very heart of the island. The sea is unforgiven and excluded from my work, though I am learning to live with it all around me.

My supposed affinity with the sea does not, at any rate, extend to taking the freight steamer in the winter — a glorified tin-can that sails once a week, piled outward-bound with potatoes and daffodil buds, and returning with tractor fuel, beer and disposable nappies. So I flew, regretting only slightly that the journey would feel too short, the transition too sudden. I need not have worried: the train broke down and sat quietly somewhere in Devon for three-quarters of an hour. I watched cows in the rain while phones chirruped manically around me; when I did get to the airport two flights were cancelled due to fog. I had time enough in the tiny departure lounge to sip plastic tea and think about the house, and wonder if he'd been much in my absence.

At the quay they loaded my suitcase and the drums of diesel and the sacks of feed and the boxes of cereal and lager and crisps onto the trailer, and George leaned down to help me up into the cab. But I wanted to walk home, slowly, through the fine rain. They overtook me, one by one, hooting, and I waved, and pressed up the gentle hill. I always forgot that it still hurt my hip to walk much, but it didn't matter. The mist was coming down here now and it was getting towards dark, and the shape of the island seemed changed.

His boots and oilskin were in the porch. They had left my suitcase just inside, and there was a damp heap of Christmas cards on the mat. I took the case up to the back room then came down and made myself pasta and lit a fire. I spent an hour or so reading through the post, waiting for the water to heat up for a bath; the wind got up outside and crackled rain at the windows. I listened to it later under piles of blankets in bed, warm, wondering vaguely if he was still somehow tuned-in to the weather even as deep down as he went, or if, for him, it was all completely calm and silent and dark. And I thought with pleasure of the morning, when I would go down to the kitchen in my dressing gown to make tea, and find on the table the white plate with the shining fish, cleaned and ready to fry, perhaps a little blue mackerel, enough for one person's breakfast. And almost better than that, the mug in the sink, and the teapot, to the touch, still faintly warm.

Nettles

He looked at gardens. Spilling with roses over low brick walls and fences onto the pavement. Twenty years ago, last year, he would have stolen one and brought it home with the bread. Different motives perhaps, but he would have done it, and felt glad to see it in the deep blue vase on the kitchen table. But not now, and he pushed the roses gently aside with his briefcase and looked over into the gardens instead. Happy daisies and huge pink mallows, blue blue delphiniums and the bonnets of aquilegia; people in this part of town let their gardens express themselves like their children, bright and disorganised, no straight edges. And his poor garden. He kept his head down as he passed the Coxes in case one of them was gardening out at the front and he had to stop to talk, to apologise, to promise another vague and untruthful date in the future.

He crossed the main road, stopped at the bakers for a loaf, and carried on up through streets of red-brick, turn-of-the-century houses, widening now, and leafier and rising. Clematis and passionflower over porches, great bushes of rosemary and lavender. A plum tree, victoria, very nearly ready; next week he would pick them up from the pavement, and put them in the pockets of his jacket, and then have to eat them as he crossed the park, throwing any over to fortune and squirrels. She had shaken and pinched all the blossom off their fruit trees that spring, and they would have none of their own.

There had been plenty of terrible scenes. They had reeled all winter from one outburst to the next, and he had been braced for each as it came, facing it as his due. He was unconditional in his surrender. There were new rules, and he agreed to them: she was to have the old playroom at the top of the house for herself alone, and he was never to set foot in it. She was to have the run of all other rooms, including his study; she could, if she wanted, read every word he wrote. He agreed to this, and when on Sundays or early before work he sat as before at his desk with the small perfect view over rooftops to the cathedral, he had felt so naked that the writing stopped. It would perhaps have stopped anyway; he was too tired.

He crossed a little road and went into the park, which began with chestnut trees, now at their fullest green. How quickly the garden had gone under. Some of it, certain roses, the big ceanothus, had been lost to violence, and some of it had pushed through anyway — all the bulbs, the impossible forget-me-nots — but her vegetable patch was soon all weeds, and the clump of nettles at the back behind the apple tree had spread confidently forward to take it. She had obliged him to let it happen. Losing the flowers broke his heart and so he accepted it as necessary suffering, but he had insisted on defending the potatoes, which mattered less, in the interests of sanity, and she had let him. But when he dug up a handful of earlies they didn't have the usual taste of victory in them, and he left the rest to rot.

After some months most of the violence had blown itself out and a sour calm set in. At first this seemed an improvement, and he felt heartened. For a while the long walk to and from work was given over to longer-term strategies, to visions of a rescued future. Retirement no longer gaped at him. At their ceremonious, mostly silent breakfasts, though her face was still washed out her eyes were no longer red. There were days of almost normality, little heavens. Summer brought the sun.

But one day he noticed her hands. She was cutting the bread, as always, very slowly and evenly, two slices each, and he saw that her hands were red. She poured milk and tea as usual, passed the shop-bought marmalade unspeaking; her fingers were swollen, and a lumpy rash flamed up her wrists.

Emma! he said, not thinking for once of his own voice hanging between them. Your hands!

She looked at them briefly: It's nothing.

But look — the rash, they're all swollen, they're all...

There is nothing the matter.

Emma, don't be idiotic, what have you done? What happened?

Nothing is wrong.

And she spread smooth butter on her bread very calmly, and wouldn't talk to him. He worried all through work, strode home in a hurry, and tried again over tea to get her to explain. They looked slightly better, but the rash was still there. That night in bed he thought of them burning and tormenting her in the dark; he woke at five to hear fine rain, and thought that it would fall on the skylight up there, gentle and cold. Perhaps she would get up in her long night-dress and let it in, holding up her poor hands to receive it.

But in the morning they were as bad again, red and flagrant. The next day was no better, and she still wouldn't talk about it, and for days he had to live helpless with worry, watching their redness; serving food at mealtimes, laying the table, drawing curtains, turning the pages of a book as they sat in the front room silently. Pushing a strand of grey hair behind her ear; stroking the cat. Throughout all this she was noticeably calmer in herself; she began to talk more, and even, after a week or so, started her Oxfam afternoon again, going off one Wednesday to sort clothes and label bric-à-brac, in cotton gloves. But the mild relenting was not much use to him under the circumstances, and at home the redness of her disfigured hands continued to accuse him.

He found himself in Boots one day on the way home. He had even left work early to get there before half five, almost unintentionally. He stood perplexed in front of shelves lined with bottles and pots of creams and lotions and did not know where to start. He felt a dizziness at the choice, and left, but came back the following day and asked the girl at the counter. Something for a rash, a bad rash. She suggested a cooling spray, but he thought a lotion would be better; not calamine, they had that. He took a white professional-looking bottle. At home he left it on the kitchen table with the bread, and said nothing. Later, clearing the table for supper, she moved it to the sideboard, and it stayed there unopened. So he tried again, a scented lotion in a nicer bottle. Then the spray. Then some after-sun soother which promised to calm and soften the most irritated skin, then some cold-cream because of the name. They lined up tidily along the sideboard, one after another.

He became a connoisseur of labels on bottles in Boots and other shops along the road he crossed to and from work. From the health-food place he bought a pot of aloe vera gel, cucumber milk, some oatmeal soap; from the New Age crystal-and-candle shop, in exquisite bottles of dark-blue glass, a number of creams in bewitching combinations: comfrey and rosewater, geranium and orange, marigold and elderflower, a witch-hazel balm. He bought convincingly-labelled German brands, and, from the Indian shop on the corner, various Oriental plant remedies whose names he had never heard of packed in coloured cardboard with information in slightly off-key English and flowing script. And because he was too shy to try the testers, not that they always had them, the walk from the road up to the park became a space of abstract, but sensuous, curiosity. He never opened a bottle to try for himself. Instead he dwelt on the names of the lotions, on their seductive pastoral or pseudo-scientific descriptions, on the thought of the leaves and petals of different plants crushed and distilled into essences. It was only half a game. The futility of it was clear from the start; she would not be tempted. Nor was he really in thrall to the evocative promises of the labels. Yet, insistent, the thought of cool white cream on those flaming hands became a sort of pleasurable obsession with him, one that he was ironically aware of, but that he permitted himself against his increasing anxiety, like moments of slack on a line getting tighter and tighter.

After a fortnight or so the sideboard became absurd. One evening when they had finished supper he quietly filled up a cardboard box and took it down to the shed, stepping carefully over the brambles that were beginning to snarl the path, brushing against the huge powdery mane of golden-rod. The door was hard to open after all this time. He put down the box and felt the gentle brush of nettles, and, a few seconds later, their itching pain. He put the box on a shelf at the back, the clean white, pink and blue of the bottles peculiar in the gathering dark. As the light outside faded he stood in the musty air, surrounded by pots and jam-jars and bits of wood, feeling his hand burn with the nettle rash and looking out of the little webbed-up window. They were as high as the window here, their black jagged heads foregrounding the rest of the garden. They spread then in large patches, clumped around the base of the apple tree, vaunting their height along the fences, across the old vegetable patch, rife at the back against the wall. The light went on in the kitchen, he could see Emma moving around, then taking up position at the sink, the garden's length away. He went back into the house and made a pot of tea.

He didn't sleep. Thoughts came at him like birds, mobbing him. By the following morning he was all numb with fatigue, and had decided to break the first and most powerful rule, the rule of her privacy. His mind flinched from the consequences. Now, the first time for ages, he had to be devious, setting off for work as usual, phoning the office from the box at the park gates to say that he would not be in until the afternoon if at all, and then waiting. He waited awkwardly at the edges of the park, feeling criminal and foolish until she appeared round the corner. She had her gloves on, and the big shopping bag, and the tired, distant look about her that made him feel unreal, as if he only existed in a place at the wrong end of the telescope. They waited about ten minutes; the bus came late. As it juddered down the hill he crossed the road and slipped home.

The playroom was unrecognisable. She had stripped it of pictures and painted it white, removed all the books and toys they kept out for their granddaughter. A low single bed (she must have lugged it out of the attic there herself) and a small table he didn't even recognise, and in the centre, under the skylight, her loom. He stepped a few paces into the room, afraid to breathe out a tangible presence. Stood there in the new whiteness, he felt quite lost, unremembered, though he had rewired and repapered it, had fitted the little house into the far alcove, had painted the bright inspired version of his own parents' farm onto the huge flat board beside it. She had stashed the board away somewhere and the house, if it was still there, was hidden behind a plain curtain. Her colourful rugs and woven animal pictures had also gone. He soon saw what was happening.

The work on the loom was a dark mass, oddly ragged. There was about a foot and a half of it done, dark and indistinguishable towards the base, greener at the top. On the small table behind was a kind of simple press made with bricks and planks and cardboard, and beside the loom on the floor were two baskets, one half full of the ragged dark stuff, the other spilling over with fresh green nettles.

The absolute shock of it made him tremble, and he backed out of the room in disbelief, calling her a fool, a fool. Down two flights of stairs and into the sunny kitchen, saying Emma, woman, what idiocy is this? What bloody fairy-tale is this? What kind of stupid bloody game? He made coffee, shaking for its warm smell like a drug, and then stood at the sink, holding the mug in both hands, staring out at the green exhilarated nettles. There were even more of them from this window than from the shed.

She came in as he stood there, still incredulous, gathering rage. His temper, that had been so heroically patient, so pliable, came furiously over him and he shouted at her, grievous bitter words. Then he went out and stormed the garden with a sickle, lashing out, waist high. The nettles lashed back. He beat them down, and trampled them, and grasped at their ugly yellow roots, tearing them up and cursing as they snapped. The smell was intoxicating, metallic, like a dozen childhood summers. When he stopped to draw sobbing breath in the midst of the mess she came out to him, and looked at him almost gently, pushing back her hair with her white-gloved hands. She told him not to waste his time. There were plenty of nettles next door, she said; and more still behind the garages at the back, and beautiful nettles down at the old railway. Don't waste your time.

She was still as distant from him as a cat, and his rage had not shaken her, had not meant a thing. But then — he realised this afterwards, sitting at the kitchen table looking at his dirty blistered hands while she put the shopping away around him — his betrayal of her privacy had not opened an abyss. He did not need to be frightened, and, though nothing had changed, there was now no secret. He did go back to work that afternoon, and when he got home he rolled up his sleeves and went out to clear a bit of ground for himself, perhaps for some new roses. She would not like it but she would not stop him, and he could keep himself busy while he waited. That night he had a lovely dream. Early early morning in the wet, everything pearled over, spiders' webs across the path along the river, a cool green smell of plants and water. In his dream he pulled two Tescos bags from his coat pockets and began to pick dock-leaves, huge and dripping. He filled his plastic bags and went home, emptied them onto the kitchen table and

began to pile them into compresses, thick and green, squeez-
ing out beads of water. Then he was up in the white room, and
Emma asleep on her back like an effigy, her shocking red hands
folded over the counterpane, perverse as a medieval saint,
and he was pressing them gently between the cool wadded
leaves.

Every day as he walked across the park he wondered
how much longer. And though he was a hopeful man, he was
tormented by possible endings. The darkest was that it would
burn him, that her revenge would be to watch it turn to snakes
around his chest. The sweetest, the hope that flickered at him
on and off, especially in dreams, was that it would change him
back into himself again, recognised, beloved. It was really towards this end that he was bit by bit reclaiming his garden,
because the third did not seem to him possible; no, it was not
possible that she would never finish, that she would ravel and
unravel, just to keep him wheeling around pointlessly in the
cold pale sky forever.

The Elephant
at Tregaron

Gwydion had pigs, hurrying north. But this lot came from the east, from the East, very slowly. And where he rushed his men to strike camp and push on, through the rain over Pumlumon, and through the forests of Gwynedd, leaving place-names like sudden indelible footprints behind them, these were painfully slow, a real palaver, and they have left almost nothing. Which is remarkable, considering their size.

They are into Cardiganshire. The wagons of Batty's Menagerie are creaking past cottages and July hedgerows, the lions and tigers and pythons and cockatoos and monkeys all jolted up and down inside. But the elephants must have been walking, lumbering along, perhaps harnessed up and pulling wagons, perhaps feeling some pleasure in the presence of the sun, smelling the summer in the hedges. People have come out of their houses to stare. It is Sunday and for once God seems good. They have made excellent progress into this wild place, which does not look so bad when the sun is out, especially the pretty hedgerows, it reminds him of Cornwall, where they were oh, seven years ago now, so long already? And see how the people are thrilled.

George Batty is the brother of the more famous William Batty, the equestrian manager who leased the big circus that had once been Philip Astley's. He is uncle to George Batty the jockey-act rider and Thomas Batty the lion-tamer (so covered in scars that, on one side of his body from the ankle upwards, a half-crown cannot be placed between them). And there is Lena Batty the equestrienne, who performed with Henglers, and Madame Frederica Batty, wife of nephew George, with her amazing dancing dog. He is vaguely proud of them all, of their total effect, of their Name, but they all get on better as individuals doing their own jobs, and his job is touring the provinces with his collection of exotic animals. It is his whole life, since Mrs Batty died. And no one, to his knowledge, has ever been this far west. He straightens up on his horse and beams at the staring people.

They halt in Tregaron, in the market square. They fill it with beasts and their minders, spilling over into the stables of the Ivy Bush and the Talbot. The wagons are pushed into the ring position and a few of the advertising boards are put up: this is only a temporary stop, overnight, but there's no point wasting an audience. *Handsome Blue Macaw (very rare); Crested Porcupine; Magnificent specimen of the Drill baboon.* It is a lovely sunny late afternoon, and Batty, having seen everything right, goes into the Talbot for a well-earned drink. They will show tomorrow morning, and then press on. *Indian and African leopards; Young Russian Bear; Dromedary; Pair of Irish Badgers; Young Lion.* A warm fug to drink in, and an audience. He does not mind not understanding the background language, the comments tossed around him, he has nothing to fear. Besides, he is doing the talking, and, he assumes, they understand him. The landlord places a tactical drink beside him at the bar, and Batty gives a gracious happy bow. *"Rajah": young Indian elephant about seven years old, very docile, trained to carry children.* He tells them of the trials of owning a travelling menagerie, of the obstacles and expenses that are his adventures. Of broken axles on wretched roads, of panic in the wagons during thunderstorms. He explains the kinds and amounts of food and attention the different animals require, and expounds on the cost of purchasing and maintaining them, of the terrible risks involved — his prime example relished the more for being the misfortune of a rival, George Wombwell, who bravely spent a thousand pounds on the first imported giraffe and employed a team of men to make it a special cage, only to have it die within three weeks of arrival. It happened. They were often weak after the journey, often sick in the first few weeks, and monkeys especially bad. Down at the docks in London though, watching them unload, that was something to see. Hoisting them off, incredible. And whoever was making money on these animals it wasn't him or his kind, oh no. Middle men. Always the same. Damned hard work at either end and them in the middle, sitting pretty.

Batty told facts like stories. He told them that monkeys were worshipped in temples in India; that the oran otan, or pongo, or Wild Man of the Woods, stood six feet tall like a hairy man and could be trained to eat with a knife and fork, and that gangs of them would not hesitate to fall upon herds of peaceful feeding elephants and drive them away with clubbed fists and pieces of wood. That sloths took on average two days to climb a tree, but that they could kick like mules, and had, moreover, such affecting countenances that they were rarely attacked, so impossible was it to look at them and not be moved with pity, especially when they shed tears. That Indian princes drank from rhinoceros horn to guard against being poisoned, and went everywhere with great troops of elephants, all decked up in silks and jewels. In the East Indies, said Batty, the male elephant is lured into captivity by the presence of four tame females, gently manoeuvred into place around him, who distract him with caresses while ropes are tied to his legs and a kind of harness fitted around his girth: thus hobbled, it is an easy matter to attach him to a tree, release his legs, and allow him to spend his fury — and what fury — in futile, terrible fits, until he calms enough to be yoked to the females and guided into his new life. Few animals are more intelligent, claims Batty, and only dogs are more obedient, than trained elephants. Tigers, on the other hand, as his brother Thomas could prove on his scarred body, are never really tamed. And as a finale, he conjures up the family, all the whip-cracking, side-stepping, brilliant Battys as if under one big roof spotlit with the band playing, surrounded by lions and tigers and little waltzing dogs, and the lovely Lena all spangled and starry prancing into the ring with a dozen horses so plumed and gilded and caparisoned it seems like a dream.

He emerges in the evening sun and stands in the doorway a while watching them all busy, his people. Then he watches the watchers. He likes children, and notices them first, then picks out a couple of pretty girls, some young men feigning a lack of interest near the camel wagon, a clutch of elderly women with knitting needles. People are leaving church and most head towards the square to have a look, even if they think they are going somewhere else.

After five minutes or so, he sees a figure walking unlike the others, with definite purpose, towards him. A clergyman in black, a black hat clenched in his hand, as tall and thin and sallow as Batty is stocky and flushed with ale. He crosses the square and stands before him a moment, tight-lipped. Then:

— How dare you, sir, how dare you.

Quietly, and with such suppressed anger that Batty is briefly taken by surprise. And it is only as the minister turns on his heel and strides off that he recovers his aplomb and pulls out his usual retort to men of the cloth.

— They are all God's creatures sir, His marvels, His wondrous creations; the people have a right to see them, any day of the week. My show is extremely Educational, especially for the children: it is God's work too, sir, in its own modest way, this exhibition...

But the clergyman went home to Aberystwyth and lay awake that night with his anger forming sentences in his head. The next day he put his indignation onto paper.

To the Editor of *The Welshman* and *General Advertiser*
Aberystwyth, July 3, 1848

Sir, — On Sunday, the 2nd instant, the feelings of the religious portion of the Welsh people in Cardiganshire, were shamefully outraged by the conduct of Batty's Company, with their caravans and their horses, and their elephants, travelling on that sacred day through a populous part of the country, disturbing the inhabitants of the different villages during the hours of divine worship.

The writer of this, who was assisting a brother clergy-man at the town of Tregaron, was an eye-witness to this shocking outrage, both in going to, and in returning from Church. Though Tregaron had never beheld such a sight be-fore, yet to the praise of the deep religious feeling which char-acterises the Welsh people, and as far as concerns the above town, to the faithfulness of the present Vicar, it is with pleas-ure I add, the Church on the occasion was well filled; still there were scores about the streets and roads, attracted by this (to them) wonderful spectacle, and drawn away from their sev-eral places of religious worship.

If Mr Batty and his company think they may desecrate the Lord's day in the Principality, and trample under foot the divine command, unheeded and unrebuked, they greatly mis-take the character of the people among whom they are; and if these facts should be generally known at their halting places, it is probable they will be made to feel their folly in a loss, which they regard, it is to be feared, at a much higher rate than the loss of God's favour.

The same night — that is, in the early hours of the morning on the third of July — young Jez comes to Batty who is snor-ing in his wagon to say that Rajah has been taken ill. Batty groans and heaves himself out of his nest of blankets, pulls on his boots and follows Jez to the stables behind the Ivy Bush. His head hurts, and he does not want to see what he sees. The elephant is on its knees and labouring to breathe, a horrible noise. The stable is warm and stinks. And there is not much to be done except douse the beast with water and wait. He props himself by the door with a pipe and considers his options for a couple of hours. The night is too hot; he chews his pipe and ignores the palpable distress of the animal and the boy. By morning, Batty knows he cannot wait.

He gives the landlord of the Ivy Bush money for his trouble. Then, without showing, and in a cumbersome kind of hurry, Batty and company pull out of Tregaron with their wagons and their billboards. They leave a big space where they have been, and soon after they go the heat breaks: rain falls on elephant-dung and camel-shit in the empty square.

The space, like all spaces left by fairs and circuses, did not take long to lose its strangeness: it came to itself soon enough. And the little town would have too, but for the elephant in the stable. Throughout a long week the people of Tregaron came to watch it die. At first there was talk of curing it, or at least of easing its affliction, as those who knew about cattle, and those who knew about horses, and those who knew about sheep, and those who knew not much about anything offered remedies, suggestions. Opinions varied as to the cause, and Batty's instructions had been vague. But after three days when it could no longer hold up kneeling and rolled onto its side there was no more talk of curing. Its stomach began to swell, with the gases trapped inside; its eyes, almost hidden in the folds of skin, had the concentrated elsewhere look of suffering things. About then, bar the odd one or two who were seriously perturbed, most of the children stopped coming because they had seen what was to be seen and got used to it, as children do.

There were jokes too, of course, in the inns and at the market, and they had never been funnier. When new drovers came into town they were, at the third or fourth pint, offered the bargain of a lifetime, a beast the size of which you never saw before, and then they were taken to gawp and shake their heads. By Thursday the lad from the Ivy Bush who had taken over from Jez was sick of them, and sick of the stench in the stable, and had to hold grimly to the thought of the small earnings he would get for the whole hopeless business. He had been so proud to inherit the job from the boy from London, whom he had admired intensely, and who had not minded repeating instructions, nor laughed at his broken English.

On Friday the *Welshman* appeared, with the clergyman's letter, and a note of awe was heard in some conversations; some of the joking took on a nervous edge. On Sunday, though the vicar, perplexed as to where he should stand on the issue, made no reference to the animal nor to the earlier indignation of his brother in God, several members of the congregation silently added it to their prayers.

The Welshman etc, July 14th 1848

Tregaron — We have this week to record a most strange and unusual occurrence in these parts, it being the decease of no less illustrious a quadruped than one of Batty's young elephants, who laboured under so severe an indisposition that the company were obliged to leave him behind at this place on Monday 3rd inst. No one in Tregaron having had any experience in attending a similar patient, we cannot confidently assert that he had the best treatment he possibly could have; we are, however, bold to say that he had the best this place could furnish, but he ceased to breathe at half-past four o clock pm on Monday last. There are many strange conjectures as to what should be done with his remains.

Illusion requires movement, and Batty was wise to rush on: *we must step on it, lads*, said Gwydion, *for the spell will not hold much longer*. If the poor beast could only have lumbered peaceably through on its way to Aberystwyth or Carmarthen or wherever they were headed next, it would have touched enough lives with a few hours' entertainment. Some of them, children perhaps, would have been deeply marked — the delicate curl of a trunk around a wrist, imagine that. Seen and touched and gone, it would have lived on like any miracle in hearts and minds for years. But for it to stop. To sink down on its knees and not get up, and to finish up somewhere as familiar as the stable behind the pub, dying of the weather or sorrow or lead-poisoning or the wrath of an unjust God, that is a cruel disenchantment for anyone to witness. The boy at the Ivy Bush put his money towards the fare to America, and swore he would not be coming back.

But the rest of the town recovered. The elephant was decently buried, and returned to its rightful sphere — the talked-of, the remembered. And the local poet, Iorwerth Glyndwr, put it very properly in an englyn:

Cawrfil! ie, dewr ac arfau! — nis gall
Ysgoi rhag saeth angau;
Ddyn balch, 'waeth ti na minnau,
Y bedd yw'n diwedd ni'n dau.

Great tusky beast! So bold — but see,
From Death's own arrow thou couldst not flee.
Proud creature, it is ever thus:
The grave will end the both of us.

And the burial? They'll tell you it's at the top of the field behind the Talbot. Unless they found a more sensible solution, you have to imagine the effort, a noble mad enterprise involving ropes and pulleys and a great deal of digging and shouting and sweating in the July sun, all culminating in a real sense of achievement, a work deserving of many pints, and a filled-in pit as deep as an elephant, levelled and soon grassed over.

It goes on a map of nameless places where the strangest things are buried, a wrecked Noah's Ark, the wasted spoils of an empire's great unfair swap, scattered wide over Wales and Britain and Europe. There are never any mounds to mark the spot, no roadsigns to keep the flicker of the past in a name. Grass, and nothing to show.

Inside

Malachy sits on the toilet which he has just cleaned, his head in his hands. It rings and rings and rings. His hands over his ears do not help: it rings through them, through the locked door, and out in the shining atrium and the white corridors he knows it is deafening, the ringing, and all he can do is wait.

When they came the first time, an hour ago, it was the Fire Brigade. He had hidden then in the broom cupboard, with his big red vacuum cleaner and his buckets and mops in the dark, and they had not found him, only his charred loaf in the microwave where he had left it to defrost, turned up full for half-an-hour while he emptied the Top Corridor's bins of brown apple cores and crisp packets and scrunched-up kleenex. Not the desks, though the same rubbish often sat absently on them among the papers and laptops, he took nothing from the desks, and he did not touch the slipping mounds of paper. He was not particularly curious about their lives, or what they did, even the ones who had photos of their children or post-cards from sunny places or pebbles and little dusty plants, but he had the evolution of all their rooms by heart. Those who endured the gradual encroachment of chaos and then purged themselves, vindicated themselves, in a sudden clean sweep, and those who could see the white surface of their desks most of the time. He liked some of them, the ones who worked late. But he liked it best when they'd gone. How quickly, spinning peacefully around in the microwave, his loaf had turned from ice to carbon. When the rough scent of smoke reached him through the disinfectant he had run down too late to stop the alarm.

They had not found him; they thought he had left. The Boss came out too, he had to, it was his responsibility, even though it meant hiking half a mile up the frozen track to the main road where he had sensibly left his car the night before, even though it meant leaving in the middle of dinner with his family, and his son just back from the States, even though it was so bloody cold. Malachy heard him say this, or bits of it, to one of the firemen as they stood outside his cupboard. Mostly he was apologetic though, and grateful for their promptness, and courteous. They had had to come out too, of course, in the same cold. Just doing our job, said the fireman. But the Boss kept thanking him and apologising, rather formally, on behalf of his staff. He probably didn't say bloody cold, he wouldn't say that. It was, though, outside the building. There was no window in the broom cupboard, but

Malachy knew that outside in the dark it was snowing very lightly.

Malachy ached from crouching in the broom cupboard, but he was phenomenally patient. Even when it all went quiet he waited a long time, flexing the muscles in his dead left leg, waiting for the silence to settle as he really knew it. No one else knew the building in the way he knew it. By eight o'clock at night, bleached and polished, it was his greatest possession. He would sometimes honour and celebrate it with a meal that he cooked himself in the kitchen downstairs. Something simple, since there was only a sink and a microwave, but always with a bottle of Italian wine which, when Somerfield or Spar permitted, came from his great-grandfather's part of Italy, from the Abruzzi, where Malachy had never been. It was a family tradition to drink wine from this region, and Malachy felt it enhanced his celebration. The bottle for tonight was not even open. The silence relaxed. He would finish the Top Corridor's bins and then drink a glass of wine to reward himself for having escaped. And then he would go home and go to bed. He did not want to eat tonight, after all.

He felt for the handle and unfolded himself from the broom cupboard. There was still a sharpness of smoke in the air, probably worse in the kitchen, but he would finish those bins first. It was dark; he knew where the stairs were, and felt for the switch at the top. But as his fingers found it he crossed an invisible watching beam: a red eye lit up on the ceiling. Light and noise exploded on him simultaneously. Pitiless, the light and the ringing together, holding him in terror in the shining atrium, bleached and polished to perfection, the alarm ringing through his whole body like Judgement Day. He stared at the big front door. The noise cut through his head. He could not remember the code he tapped in every day, and it was too late. This time it would be the police, they would be halfway across town, and the Boss would soon be trudging up his icy track in righteous anger and disbelief. Panic, the sheerest wave of it, carried him downstairs to the toilet. He sat with door locked covering his ears against the cruel ringing, and knew that this time they would be quicker to find him.

On the Ground

We laughed at them together, but when my husband left me I found the Welton Ramblers both kind and supportive. One of them would ring me the day before their walks to persuade me to come along, and I usually did. Grief, you might think, should recoil from bonhomie and gaiters, and it is true that it was always an effort to make it to the designated car park by ten, always an effort to watch them tumble smiling out of cars and put their shining boots on, then to get out myself and be greeted with a warm pat on the back. But the walking was a great help, and I hadn't the courage or energy to do it alone. I should have got a dog to replace my husband I suppose, but

I hate the smell of them.

At fifty-five I was the youngest, and they liked me for being New Blood. The oldest, though she died two or three weeks after I started, was eighty-nine and needed a lot of help with stiles. There were a couple of others in their eighties but most were late sixties, mid-seventies, retired, with grandchildren about whom we heard a lot. I learned to walk in a flock, to appreciate the dynamics of conversation on the move, perpetually altering with the nature of the path and the places we went through – the quiet one-to-one conversations with a degree of intimacy, the loud cheery discussions along little metalled lanes, the banter of the bottlenecks at stiles and gates. And up and down the straggling line, orders: to turn right or left, to wait for people to catch up, to stop for coffee (milky out of flasks, with homemade cakes), or Comfort Breaks (gentlemen forward please, ladies behind this hedge). There were yellow arrows and friendly acorns on every gatepost. And it happened too that there were moments like bubbles when you could float along in the middle, supported but untouched, briefly alert to the background of it all, the smell of leaf-mould or the colour of a field. Mill-ponds, ivied walls, yew hedges, a red wheelbarrow, accumulating in my head in broken images. Once a week for four or five months, and soon I wasn't the main magnet for tactful sympathy, soon there were other tragedies, more serious than mine. And then I too was shaking my head and talking in a low voice about Elizabeth's poor husband, while Elizabeth marched on bravely up ahead.

I knew I was truly one of the group when they invited me on the annual Rambling Holiday in September. They had booked all the rooms in an old vicarage, now run as a B&B, in mid-Wales. There was no coach; we all had to make our own way there, and I was lucky that the Rushtons offered me a lift.

The days were structured around walks, but flexible enough for people to go sightseeing. The evenings we were all together in the dining room (lace, mahogany, third-rate landscapes by a local artist) for long convivial meals with entertainment on two nights after supper.

I didn't tell anyone until we got there that my mother was Welsh, that, though I grew up in Yorkshire, we came to Wales to see cousins on their farm every year, perhaps not far from where we were staying, I wasn't sure any more. When that got around I was marked out for special attention, half-flattering, half-teasing, and treated as a native guide: I was held personally responsible on the few occasions it rained, and blamed for the extravagance, and possible danger to motorists, of bilingual roadsigns. Not quite truthfully (there were fragments still, from Mam and the cousins), I denied all knowledge of the language; but they made me pronounce the place-names, and then laughed and did it their way. John needed sunshine and we always holidayed in white villas in the olive groves of Greece and Spain: I hadn't been to Wales for years and years.

I thought something might happen, therefore, and was partly expectant, partly braced against it. A return to the landscape of childhood, to a landscape of the heart, ought to have some effect on the heart even at its deadpoint, even in hibernation. The first day passed smoothly enough, with a simple circular walk close to our vicarage. I felt calm, dreamy, but acknowledged a few sharp flickers of recognition at the rowans with their glorious berries and the extraordinary effect of light and cloud on the hills around us. I slept beautifully.

Then things began to get complicated. At first, it was still nothing to do with me: we simply lost the path. Or rather, as our flustered leaders put it, the map just did not match the reality on the ground. It took about twenty extra minutes and a couple of awkward fences before the world and the map fell back into their places, faithful reflections of one another. The episode rattled the leaders, and there was a moment of unusual tension at supper, quickly damped by embarrassed partners. The rest of the group, once safely back and after a cup of tea, congratulated themselves on the adventure, and felt rather proud.

But then it happened again, twice, on the next walk: rusted double barbed wire where there should have been a stile, and, an hour later, a muddy ditch cutting right across the path. They could not be expected to climb or jump at their age, and the long trek round to find alternative routes, across marshy uneven grass highly treacherous to ankles, added about three-quarters of an hour to the whole walk and wore the older ones out. I was not especially tired, and talked cheerfully with the best of them: and yet there was a moment, as I helped Mrs Ellis across a particularly difficult bit of bog, when I heard a dog barking from the nearest farm, and felt fear lay a gentle hand, very briefly, on my shoulder.

Back home this time there was outrage at the violation of our rights of way: everyone wanted to see the relevant section of the map with its brave pink dotted lines. That those lines had been worth nothing on the ground was upsetting, and it was not surprising that there was a sharp exchange or two at the dinner table. The next day was a rest day, and everyone was encouraged to go off and find waterfalls, tearooms and antiques, leaving behind a small group, who, in a council of war after the harp-playing the night before had decided on a plan to split up and walk the last two days' routes to avoid any further distress. Though there were several kind offers I had decided against tagging along with the Rushtons or the Willises or anyone else, and so found myself, a relative newcomer, sharing anxieties with the inner group. And then there I was, teamed up with Geoff and Barbara, strapping on a small rucksack containing a picnic, an anorak, and for the first time, my own map.

He was a retired headmaster and she had run the town library for years, yet neither appeared to have any problem including me, who had done nothing very much for so long now. We're impressed with how well you've coped, said Barbara. You've been a real asset to the group, said Geoff. I told them how much they'd all helped me. Our path climbed alongside a stream through a forest of small twisted oaks with mossy trunks and glowing orange leaves, with flashes of blue sky up ahead. It's good to start by going uphill; it gets the blood going. Everything looked sharp, the shadows and the rocks and the water, somewhere between the experience of pure mental lucidity and having the optician ratchet up your vision another notch. They told me about their daughter who had married an Italian, and I told them how Andrew had changed his mind about university at the last minute and gone off to Thailand, and how he seemed not to want to come back. They said not to worry, that it wasn't my fault, and that he would come back when he was ready. The wood opened out; we passed a ruined cottage with four mature ash trees planted rather poignantly around it, and let the path take us upwards towards the hills. After perhaps another hour of gentle climbing in open country we stopped to eat our packed lunch out of the wind, sitting in a row against a stone wall and looking down the valley with satisfaction. I felt like laughing.

On a day like this day there seemed no reason to ever stop the gentle, compelling climb towards the big hills, but our walk now turned us away from them, down into the next valley, beginning the loop back to the cars. There was more woodland, a straggle of birch and rowan around a darker plantation of firs. The path predictably lost its nerve around here, and seemed to give up; but a quick reconnoitre found it again down the far side of the trees, where we picked up a farm track heading in purposeful zigzags down towards some outbuildings.

And then, confusion. The track stopped at a couple of stone sheds with rusted corrugated iron roofs. Around them, picturesque and unsettling, nettles and decaying machinery, and no sign of a way through. We did a circuit as far as we were able, scouted briefly to either side, and then sat down on the bottom step of a small flight leading up to nowhere. Geoff sat in the middle and smoothed the map, and we all tried to make sense of what we could see. I've never been any good at contours, so I mostly kept quiet as they pointed and pored, trying to get the landscape to fit. The plantation behind us was part of the problem, since it seemed to be the wrong shape and obscured the edge of the hill, but the complete disappearance of the track was more disconcerting. It should have led down to a farm: Barbara thought she could see a roof, but where the path should have been was thick with brambles and a rotting wire fence that looked as if it had been there for years.

We had tea from a flask, and Geoff came up with a plan. The way we intended was clearly impossible, but there were various options from where we stood. To save time and energy each of us would take a different route, and walk for fifteen minutes — absolutely no more — in that direction, stopping as soon as we were confident of our bearings and could see a plausible way of rejoining the walk. If this happened in the first five minutes, we could shout; otherwise we were to meet back at the steps in half an hour. I did not like this plan at all. I tried to ask if I could stay with Barbara, but phrased it so badly they misunderstood, and the next thing I knew we had synchronised our watches, double-checked our (probable) location on the map, and headed off. My route looked the least likely to come near the farm, and I was deeply grateful for that. I kept turning round to watch them; Barbara, in her bright yellow top, turned once and waved. Then she went round a corner, and Geoff disappeared into the trees, and the fear came swooping back. This time it put both arms around me and gave me a tight, cold hug.

I wouldn't do it. I could follow my wall up to the right and stop at the brow of the hill and wait there until they came back. There was no need to lose sight of the outbuildings. The sun was still shining, and I would be fine. The fear let go, slipped a chilled hand into mine, and we both set off. Onwards and upwards, I said to it, onwards and upwards. But the fear was in a mood to reminisce.

What came back first had already been triggered by the barking dog the previous day. We were climbing a track, my father just ahead of me. We had lost the path, and he was taking a chance on a short-cut up to the road through a farm, which meant that we were trespassing, a dreadful word, and I was frightened. In my head I practised words in Welsh to show the angry farmer when he came that we were sorry, that we had made a mistake, and that most important of all we were not tourists. *Ar goll. P'nawn da. Flin gen i. Ar goll.* And the name of the cousins' farm as the ultimate protection, *Hafod Isa, Hafod Isa*. The farm was ramshackle, the outer sheds had broken windows. A dog on a chain saw us and went berserk. I kept close to my father and we walked through the yard. There was man sitting on the steps outside the farmhouse with a thick yellow telephone directory open on his knee. He wore a sawn-off T-shirt with a union jack; his hair was cropped very short and his face was brutal. He did not look up. The dog whined and twisted on its chain as we walked through quickly up to the track.

The fir plantation behind me presumably brought back a second memory, a single image. This time we were walking across moorland towards the dark edge of a pine forest that blocked the horizon to the left. As we walked, someone came out from the trees onto the horizon and stood there for a minute or two, a black figure holding a long gun. My father, as usual, did not break his stride, and neither of us said anything, though I pushed my hand gently through the crook of his arm, much as the fear held mine now, and tried to keep step across the heather. When we reached the ridge the man had gone.

And the third. More open land, straggling trees, perhaps birches, some gorse in flower. It was mizzling rain, and we saw up ahead an incongruous wooden shed with a rusty zinc roof. Like an outbuilding that had drifted from its home farm, miles from anywhere. It might do to eat lunch in, he said, and pushed on ahead of me to see. I stopped to tie a bootlace, and by the time I straightened up he was on his way back to me. Locked, he said curtly, and took my arm, pulling me along too fast. I glanced over to the shed and saw a yellow face at the little window, and heard a low moaning. I didn't ask questions, I kept going, sick with terror. We never said a word.

There was probably more to come but by then the fear and I had got to the edge of the hill. I looked back down to the outbuildings: they were still there. I checked my watch: I had done five minutes of my fifteen. The fear wandered off into the bracken and I took a deep breath, got my map out and looked around me. To my absolute astonishment there was a stile at the far of end of the field, about fifty yards way, and an old wooden signpost with most of the words *Llwybr Cyhoeddus* still legible, pointing down a green lane. I followed it.

At first it was just one, a three-wheeled Robin Reliant in a distinctive 1960s pale blue, tipped on its side in a field to my right. Then there were two or three more, broken up, in a heap of primary colours to the left; then a rusting tractor, and half a white van. And as the beautiful lane curved ahead of me there were more and more, until I was looking across a small valley with a stream running down past two or three thorn trees, dotted with sheep and clumps of rushes and innumerable three-wheelers, old Fiestas, bisected tractors, rusted engines, wheels and doors, partly hidden by, partly rising from the bracken like dead or sleeping animals, and in such amazing colours, such washed-out reds and greys, rusts and yellows and more of that unmistakeable blue that it took my breath away. They were scattered exactly as though they had been rubbish left by a glacier, dense in the cup of the valley and thinning gradually towards the top where the real hills began. And I knew then that what I wanted most of all was to stand at the head of the valley and look down on them in the yellow afternoon sun. I stuffed the map back into the rucksack and swung it onto my back and set off up the hill with such energy that I knew the fear would have a job to keep up. I reckoned I'd probably beat it to the top.

Kissing Swallows

I know how old she is, and think she looks well on it. Thick curly honeybrown hair which she doesn't always tie back, it falls across the page sometimes; she twists it round her finger. When she walks from the issue desk with her stack of books the automatic doors spring open for her and all the heads in the reading room raise up, take her in, rejoice. And then they are vague again, bent to their work. Except him, with his radar, he'll have spotted her before the doors opened and will have been frowning deep into his laptop, looking anywhere but up, and still somehow knowing where she sits (she favours seven, and twenty-seven, but she is not consistent) and when it is safe to glance over, long after her entry is forgotten. His self-control is phenomenal. I know how old he is too and he doesn't look a day less. Younger than she is, and young to be so grey, but tall, and craggy as a cliché. Heads go up for him too, and he knows it. Let them work, if they can, I have things to do myself. Requests to process, a missing order, the new and precarious computer system to coax.

I let Nia go for coffee first, which is usual; they generally show no sign of moving before eleven. And I give them a minute's head start, so I can pick my place accordingly, although hazard always has a part in this, which pleases me — I don't push it. Because if I tried to control it every time, can you imagine, the frustration, being in the wrong place in the queue, the perfect table occupied by a couple of toothy Americans researching their Welsh roots, the sun tempting her out for a fag, no, I let hazard decide if it is a good day or a bad, and I say there will always be other days, I do not let it spoil things. I imagine they do the same.

Of all the floor-shows I have watched and continue to watch every working day theirs is the subtlest, the most aesthetically pleasing, and the longest running. What is it now, three, four years? Four years measured out in coffee spoons, but oh, Mr Eliot, there is no ennui here. I did actually keep count for a while, until she got ill and he had a sabbatical in the States and it rather skewed the statistics, but at one point I could have told you: *fact*, eight times out of ten they ignore each other magnificently. It is a joy to watch. He often has a newspaper to hide in. She seems to know everyone, and either joins laughing groups, or has intimate, animated one-to-one discussions with friends. But she is careful to sit in his line of vision, or what would be his line of vision if he were ever to look up, lifting a coffee cup absently, miles away, to sweep the place with a gaze so vague the café could be empty of souls. And not a flicker as his eyes move across her, not one. You would not notice what he notices, but I do. He knows her pretty necklaces off by heart. She fetches an unnecessary glass of water; her skirt swings.

Back at the issue desk I find I am on top of things. It is wonderfully quiet today. I let Eleri mind the handful of docile readers and do some catching up. Her latest article has finally arrived, why it takes them so long to process journals I'll never know, and I settle to read, a year later, what I helped her to write. I read the footnotes first and remember the highlights: the big brown-leather three-tome monster that made her gasp the first time she saw it. I would not let her carry it. The tiny, beautifully-illustrated nineteenth-century guide to the Bay of Naples that made her murmur with delight. A flashy, recent monograph that irritated her, I could tell by the length of time she took over it and her expression when she gave it back. Articles by friends and colleagues from Oslo, Manchester, LA (when I have plenty of time on my hands I work out, from the conferences she has attended and the dates of her employment in previous institutions, which of the people she reads she is at all likely to know). And when I have recalled what I can of the process of writing it, I read her piece, admire her prose, enjoy her fine turns of phrase — clear thought with occasional arabesques, like a skirt swinging. And I thank my stars again that she works on something that makes sense to me. She was a leading glaciologist in her time, one of those blamed and admired women who leave young families to go on dangerous expeditions; she lost a finger to frostbite, on her left hand. Her early stuff is dazzling, but hard for me to follow. Now she works more on the history of the subject in general I can follow along behind her, invisible, treading where she treads.

I have low expectations of lunch. Too many people; it tends to the chaotic and the noise is often too much for me to keep an eye on anything, although the chaos works to their advantage sometimes, it seems to relax things a little. Once in a while two glances will skim across the tables, barely flickering as they cross, faster than swallows in flight. Oh Julia, I tease them in my head, oh Winston. A point to me.

Throughout the sleepy afternoon I get things done well enough. Between tasks I reward myself by checking through his catalogue to see what he's reading. His work interests me less, and I do not follow it closely, but he's a ferocious reader, I'll give him that. Six out again today, and four will be stripped of what he needs by closing time. There is something ruthless about the way he works, which is probably why, very, very occasionally, I throw him a provocation, call up something in his name to sit innocently in his pile of jargon-ridden works on sociology: a pocket-sized illustrated edition of the German *Minnesänger*, a little jewel. I watched him turn it over in his hands, briefly and pleasantly intrigued. Another time, more maliciously, it was *Teach Yourself Welsh*. He's a Valleys boy, can't see the point, and until recently used to bristle at my quiet, insistent courtesies. But perhaps she's having an effect there too; she's a good Scandinavian of course, and her Welsh is excellent. And when he brought it back to the desk and said there had been a mistake it was a pleasure to swivel the screen round and show him exactly when he ordered it, his number and so on, and watch him flush at my jokey suggestion that he'd perhaps called it up subconsciously. Of course I then blamed our neurotic computer system and said that these things happen.

It still surprises me how physically demanding intensive

reading can be. You can see it in their eyes by tea time; and their outlines look blurred, dishevelled. It makes them vulnerable. If it is going to happen, the rare event, it is most likely to be over tea, a few words at the machine, a courteous may-I-join-you, and a few inconsequential phrases thrown a little awkwardly like the first lines of silk from a spider — until one sticks, and they start passing the thread back and forth, and the air around them is full of patterns all shimmering, all invisible. You could not simply call this conversation. I hold my breath and bow my head over the little teapot and feel only awe as they spin silver around each other, wrapped in a twenty-minute shining oblivion. Little wonder they spend most of their time avoiding each other, like magnets facing the wrong way; you could not live with this every day.

I have sometimes wondered if they know each other better somewhere else, outside the Library, if they have walked and eaten and slept together in another world, real or virtual. Once, heavily disguised, I went looking for them in cyberspace but found it deeply unsettling, full of monsters, and have not been back. As for the real one: supermarkets? Garages? I do not want to think of her, nine-fingered queen of the bluegreen glaciers, there. I have, I admit, hovered like an angel a few times over her house using Google Earth, but I do not follow her around streets and shops and car-parks, I am no sordid stalker. Besides, I am quite certain that the perilous tension between them thrives on an intermittent and uncertain intimacy, and can never be acknowledged by either side.

I sit over the empty teapot, perfectly still, until I hear the scraping of chairs; then I watch them pull apart, snapping the tiny threads with some effort. And I am back at the issue desk — brownsuited and unnoticed, a cross between Philip Larkin and the Bwa Bach — well before their separate returns, aloof and preoccupied, each trailing little silver filaments. Oh Dafydd, oh Morfudd, you have birch leaves in your hair. She packs up almost at once, hands me her books distracted, her thanks automatic, and is gone. He sits at his desk with his head in his hands for a full five minutes before starting again and sticking it out, like me, until closing time.

And so it could have gone on, another four years at least, had not Management in its infinite wisdom decided otherwise. That fragile, nervous computer system does not now, it seems, require my attention; it has grown up, flexed its muscles, taken on responsibilities. My knowledge of the archives, of the precious books themselves, is no longer required. Perhaps I am not deemed efficient, who knows; experience, even thirty years of it, is not enough. What happens to people like me when they leave the Library I do not know, but it will not be many weeks now before I find out.

I do not deny that it is a destructive act, but they are my story and I will finish them before I go. There will be a day when they come in to work as usual, and settle at their tables with their laptops and their piles of books, glancing just once across the reading room to check that the other is there. She will push her honeybrown hair back over her shoulder and open her book, and sooner or later they will each find a postcard with their name on, a date and a time and a website address. The postcards will be beautiful. I think they will be of the kissing swallows from the old frescoes in Santorini. The website will exist for a few hours only, and will contain this story. Oh Paolo, oh Francesca, enjoy the read.

Hard as Hail

When it rains on that roof it sounds as hard as hail. And when it hails it is like gravel and nails fired from guns, guns fired from heaven. But she has put net curtains in the shed window and at last there are three breeze-block steps up to the side door, because temporary, as she should remember from the last time, is often a long time, is often years. She is now about a hundred yards from the first house he built them, a nice enough bungalow with a lot of roof space and a big window at the back looking down across the marshy fields to the sea. They lived in a tiny caravan while he worked on the house, and it took much longer than expected because of the money and the problem with his brother, and it felt even longer than that because she hated her job as a dinner lady, because they bullied her, because he bullied her, and because it was cold. The doctor said it was a breakdown. She carried the word around like a lucky charm, and after she got better and the house was eventually finished and she found a cleaning job up at the hospital she would drop it into conversation, *pan ges i'r brêcdown*, to buy a moment or two of respect. The house was nice and she liked keeping it clean, she really did. So what, everyone wondered, must she feel like looking across from the big metal shed, pulling back the lace a little to watch the new owners pottering in the garden.

Eventually, and again it took much longer than expected because of the money and the problem with the builders, eventually she couldn't look across at the first house any more, because the second one had started to rise up between them. Much bigger, just like he said. Bigger than the big metal shed he said he needed for his work but which they had been living in the back of for at least a year while the village speculated about their plumbing arrangements and the legality of it all. Big and square, with lots of rooms, although it was not entirely clear why they might need so many. And then, to general satisfaction, it stopped halfway up for about six months, a jagged square of breeze blocks with holes where the windows should be, rained on, commented on by those who passed in the normal course of things, walking a dog, pushing a baby in a pram, moving livestock or shifting feed, running after a small boy on a bike. The English architect who lived the other side of the big shed added the concrete half-house to the other angry scars on his heart and planted a forest of small trees against it, willing them to grow. He kept his eyes straight ahead when passing, but everyone else, even those in cars, had a good look and an opinion. The general consensus was that he had run out of money again, in spite of the huge profit he must have made on the bungalow. Or that he had quarrelled again with the builders. Somebody said he'd been seen at a car boot sale selling off the tools of his trade; but someone else saw him much in demand at a craft fair, and business, so he said to them, had never been better.

As most people in the village knew by now, whatever they, or more usually the postman, got from him was not likely to be the truth. There was in some quarters a kind of exegetical tradition devoted to interpreting the real state of affairs behind any statement either of them might make. If business was thriving he was probably crippled with debt; the arm she showed someone, bruised dark down its whole length, was hardly likely to be a fall against a cupboard. He was still a ready talker, given the chance, his fluent affability laced with poison against anyone except the person he was talking to, but she now seemed to be thoroughly inarticulate in both languages, which interfered with each other to the point where neither really worked, odd in her English and now cut off from the resources of her family over the hill by some horrible feud. So as often as not she kept a moody silence, looking black as hell at you as she walked past with the dog, in the days when they still had a dog.

She lost her job at the hospital and got one at an old people's home. He encouraged her to work more shifts than she could really manage, more than anyone could manage. They must have needed the money, after all. She didn't much like this job either, having little inclination to the sunny patter used on the inmates and finding no natural allies among the other staff. But she worked hard, as always, fuelled by a kind of general resentment and perhaps by fear of him; perhaps by the promise of the big house, the promise of something better. *Dwi eisie mynd adre*. I want to go home, said the old man, again and again. *Nôl i'r tŷ*. When can I go? She usually managed to ignore him. He wore a heavy tartan dressing gown and had a horrible smell and kept up a continual pathetic shuffle with his walking frame from chair to bed to window. At the window, every time, he would look out across the outbuildings to the trees the other side of the road and say he wanted to go home. *Fydd hi ddim yn hir nawr*, she would say, for something to say. It won't be long; not long now. But things always took much longer than you thought.

She was not very interested in him or any of them, but the other girls talked. Unlike the other inmates who looked out of windows and claimed the first house they could see as home the shuffling man really did come from just over the road. You couldn't see the house, they said, it was hidden up a footpath in the woods and when the walkers had found him, on a rotting mattress, apparently dying, it was filthy. Jagged holes in the thin glass of the windows. A cupboardful of out-of-date tins. Sour milk on a peeling sill, bits of newspaper everywhere, and a grubby lino covering the old black-and-reds. The setting, though, was idyllic, on a slope under the tough little oak trees that turn such an astonishing green in spring.

Between the house and the old people's home lay the sharp bend of a busy A-road, treacherous as a river in spate.

When can I go home?

Fydd hi ddim yn hir.

For several weeks she battled on, silent and angry and very tired. Then one day, at a particularly unlikely time of year when the sycamore leaves on the huge trees they had not been allowed to chop down had got the black spot and started collecting in mildewed heaps on their drive, the mixer started up again and the new house began to rise from where it had left off, until it had a roof and pvc windows (disproportionately small, some thought) and an ugly glass and metal door. The breeze blocks were plastered smooth and the whole thing was painted a shade of pale lilac that further wounded the English architect (who couldn't, after all, manage to keep his eyes averted). He tried to console himself with half-a-dozen larches, but there was not much room left in his forest, and he feared they wouldn't thrive.

And next, filling the gap between the sycamores where the old hedge used to be, an arched double gate in a cold grey metal with more than a hint of the asylum about it; padlocked too, in a village where people still left their doors not just unlocked but in summer, weather permitting, wide open. This was an enormous mystery, thought by some to be connected to the feud with her family, or was it that he wanted to keep something safe, something valuable, although it was hard to imagine quite what. The inside of the house did not look very finished, and there was no sign of the net curtains coming down in the shed.

The wind blowing round that shed at night, what must it sound like, the wind full of rain gusting across the marshy land from the sea. Lonely and dangerous, like being on an oil rig without comrades or alcohol, and you can't watch telly all night: at some point you have to lie down in the dark and feel its force against the flat metal, pushing at the roof. How she must have wanted those three or four days in the year when snow falls onto even ugly roofs like a blessing, intensely quiet in its falling, and gentle, and the next day all the lanes are white and nobody thinks to go to work. But it was always raining, drumming on the metal roof, and there was always work to go to.

And then, a For Sale sign. It would not after all, he said, be practical for them to live in the new house, just the two of them, with no family, and the money they were bound to make on the deal would more then repay the disappointment, would set them up nicely. A new start somewhere. It was what she deserved.

Night shift. The old man was at his window again looking out into the dark. When I am going back? he said. *Dwi eisie mynd yn ôl i'r tŷ.*

It's raining, she said, speaking directly to him for the first time. You can't go back in the rain. And it's dangerous. He looked at her then, and smiled slyly, patting the pockets of his dressing gown. *'Gen i fara,* he said. Bread. It keeps you safe. And he pulled a couple of old crusts out to show her, stuffing them back protectively at the flicker of disgust on her face. You should throw that away, she said. *Ych-a-fi.*

Bara, he said again. Keeps you safe.

Not against cars taking the bend at sixty, she thought. Not against the cold rain. Not against heart failure and pneumonia. Not against the muddy path, the fall, the shattered hip.

Ych-a-fi, she said again, and went off to clean the toilet. It was after midnight. They were short staffed for the third night running, but it was very quiet, easy enough. She was pretty well done, and with twenty minutes to spare. The other woman on duty, pregnant, permanently exhausted, had already fallen asleep over a cup of tea in the kitchen. Only the rain noises, the distant revving of a fridge, the swoosh of a car, and her own breathing as she cleaned vigorously, mindlessly, emptied of feeling. Then she heard the shuffling. By the time she came out he had made it into the lobby, clunking his frame along, muttering and determined. Am I going home now? he asked. *Pryd ga'i fynd adre?*

Fydd hi ddim yn hir, she said automatically, and went into the kitchen to sign off. Gemma was still asleep and didn't respond when she said she was going, that she had to go now, and that the old man was out in the lobby waving his stinking crusts. As she fetched her coat she remembered, brokenly, the thing with the bread: it was supposed to be protection against, well, Them. Fair ones; little people. Whatever you like to call them. Oh try it then, you old fool, she thought grimly, walking deliberately past him and out to the car park leaving the front door ajar. Just try it. *Fydd hi ddim yn hir.*

The Growth of
Stone

He crosses the poor dead cobbles of his London street. The porter has collected his cases and his box. His mother, housekeeper and cat are, like his flock, left now to their own devices. The glass and the little hammer feel safe in his breast pocket. His fingers lightly touch marble, Portland stone, the cracks between bricks as he passes. Four weeks and the West stretch out ahead of him full of light and promise.

Twenty minutes later he is on the coach to Bristol, jolted and free, his eyes closed in a prayer of thanks and his left hand curled round a lump of red serpentine in his pocket. His first prayer as always is for his dearest friend and teacher, whose death somehow makes no difference after the years of dying, and whose gift now makes this journey possible. Owen knows he will continue to write to him as before. It is the only way he has ever been able to explain himself to himself. His second prayer is for his mother, his housekeeper and his cat; his third for a safe journey. After a moment he adds a fourth, asking the Almighty to keep an eye on his flock. And then he watches the countryside jolt past the window, and settles his mind to sink down deep into the theory once again, to explore it slowly, methodically, in all its different aspects; to apprehend its beauty.

Hotwells was busy with *beau monde*, different from his coffee-house companions in London. It was not at all disagreeable, he was amused and sometimes flattered by the people he met here. He joined the more energetic parties for riding on the Downs, the distant Welsh hills looking lovely in the setting sun. He took the waters assiduously, noting their delicate soft milky taste. He talked to ladies with digestive problems and old gentlemen with gout: he asked for their experiences, recorded their stories of recovery and alleviation. He was convinced. Experimenting under somewhat straitened circumstances, he boiled enough of the stuff to prove to his own satisfaction that the virtue of the water was inherent in itself, and not due to any identifiable residue. The marriage of rock and water is healthy all ways round, he wrote rather smugly, for the water and for the rock. From his neat little lodgings in Castle Street he organised the necessary expeditions, up around Clifton, onto Durdham Down and Leigh Down, and out to the pits near Redland. On three separate occasions he had the breath knocked out of him with astonishment and awe: the first, standing by the Avon at the bottom of the great Gorge itself, looking up; the second, standing on the edge on the Clifton side, looking down. The third was when Mr Rowley showed him a Cotham stone, sliced in half and polished to reveal a filigree landscape, a delicate tracery of trees, shrubs and hedges, with brooks and rivers running among them. And all the knowledge he acquired gave his theory strength.

What I have found, he told his dead friend and teacher, what I have found in the quarries and on the downs, and even in the walls of buildings around me, is a truth so evident I am constantly amazed at our collective blindness. And I have tested it all the ways you showed me, in the mind, and with the hammer and the glass and the flame, and it has always come out the same; and I see it all around, but most plainly in this blessed part of the country.

His friend would smile at that, and tell him again that Dorset is the only place for stone.

Take any piece, he went on, any natural lump of rock and split it. You will know at once if it is healthy and sound inside, it will have sort of brightness within. Note that the outside has a dullish look; this is the coat, the crust, or preserving layer. What makes the coat of a stone? A mineral solution, which washes around the rocks, filling in the irregularities, binding it safe like a skin or a bark. The stone can only thrive as long as this coat is upon it. At the Redland pit I saw lumps of rock which must have come naked out of the quarry as chippings and rubble fifty years ago, some of which had grown the coat and become perfect, healthy stones. Protected thus, they can live for a long, long time.

The truth is always beautiful. As the notes piled up he imagined them on his teacher's desk, the window opened to breeze and sunshine, the papers held down by a specimen or two, and the fine head bent intently over his neat sentences and drawings. He would not hear the children in the garden, the nursemaid, the volleying calls; his long fingers would be tapping gently.

But in the same quarry, Owen wrote, there were other stones which, perhaps because of their position, had been less evenly covered by the mineral solution; had been prevented from acquiring the protective covering and had gone off, rotted. Rotten stone crumbles, it has no brightness; once its coat has been breached the air and the sun and the rain will take it in turns to destroy it. I saw this time and again; I tested it. And wherever I found the stone quite soaked through in the earth; that is, when it always continued wet in its natural bed, it had lost its bright lively colour; its ring or sound was gone; its health and strength greatly impaired; it had a pale deadish look and was, for the most part, gone or going off apace.

He wrote in the margin then: Oh my friend.

And he cannot now remember if he was there, or only thought he was, on the chair by the bed in the darkened room where the women came and went and the fingers on the counterpane grew thinner and tired, and tapped less.

When the time came to return he packed the books and specimens carefully into boxes and sent them home with the notes that would never be sent to Dorset. They went direct, but he took his time, stopping for two nights at the inn in Avebury to explore the great stones there. He tapped and tested and found it hard to make up his mind, but was inclined to agree with the local people that they were probably natural, and not, as Stukeley would have it, the monumental remains of a druid temple. What he had really come to see lay over the hill, and on the second day he took two men from the village and set off at a good pace, sunshine and poppies keeping his spirits up. At the brow of the hill he looked back at the big stones, and considered changing his mind about the temple. Then he pressed on, talking sometimes aloud to the men, sometimes silently to his friend, and occasionally, enjoying the exercise, not at all. With his tall stick in his hand he was the first to reach the place where the rough road meets the head of the flat valley, and he looked down, like the good shepherd he would never be, on the greywethers scattered below him.

They rested in the daisies and the long grass between the may trees. The effect was not stupendous, but one of growing awe, as more and more of them appeared, singly, or in companiable groups. For four hours he moved amongst them, looking through the glass and tapping with the hammer, getting the men to dig under them, measuring and sketching. They all had their proper coats, looked healthy and strong. When the men stopped for bread and cheese he asked them what they thought. Both believed, as he now did, that they had their rise there, that they grew slowly from the earth, were natives of the place; one of the men had an uncle who said they had grown appreciably in his lifetime. He sent the men home with the specimens and more than a day's wages. Alone then, he walked for a while without thinking of anything through the long grass and the evening insects and the sleeping stones. At last he chose one to sit on, and took out his notebook. He wrote for a long time then in the failing light, glancing up only once to catch sight, as he thought, of a slim familiar figure disappearing down the valley. He raised a hand, and bent back to his writing.

Noise

She keeps the telly turned up. Not for the company, she has never needed it like that; nor, particularly, to drown out the baby yelling, although it sometimes happens that way. It is to smother the crash of collapsing metal from the vast scrap heaps down at the docks, where, during working hours at least, the diggers scoop and pour unrecognisable bright objects like so much sand into huge piles for the boats to take away. It happens from the kitchen window, and the lounge, which both look down across the docks and to the huge Severn beyond. She and the whole row of council houses audience to the noise, all day every day, and too loud to get used to; something like the noise of gravel being poured into a tin cup, over and over again. If it's fine at five, five-thirty, she will turn the telly off and open the front door to let the air and the quieter sounds in. But of course with his teeth the baby cries more in the evenings anyway, and real peace is, just now, very hard to find.

She hadn't wanted quiet till she couldn't get it any more. Quiet was an unnatural state; it happened when things went wrong. At home, where the telly was always on, she couldn't do homework without music, she waited for the bus plugged into her CDs, she talked incessantly on the phone; traffic went down their street all the time. Exams intimidated her most by their weird silence, the silence of all those people breathing. But this noise is different, it is relentless, crushing, and it fills her days. The row of houses is the rim of the bowl of noise; sound carries across from the docks, amplified, theatrical, closer than it is. Most people in the row, she thinks, must be away during working hours, and those that are left are probably old and deaf. When she and the baby were relocated, after Stuart went to prison, she was delighted with this haven, and showed it off to her mum, her sister, and to the friends who made the effort down from town. Less and less often, she can see that now, even her mum. The buses are useless.

Chipped nail, snagging; she bites it, though she ought to file it and start again with the varnish, get Mandy over to help do them for her, a new colour. He'll wake any minute. She gets his bottle. Then they must go. When a woman she met through Alison had suggested some cleaning, subcontracted in a way that wouldn't interfere with benefits, she took it as a chance to get out. And there were no buses involved because it was up the canal towpath, one of the holiday cottages tucked away behind the lock. She walks up that way a lot anyway, pushing the pram down past the docks then up and out over the ridge, like coming out of a pool, you almost expect your ears to go pop. In a year or two he will insist on staying at the heart of the noise to watch the grabbers and the trucks, will wrap fat fingers round the railings of the crane graveyard, where skeletons pile up green yellow orange red blue like a giant Lego set, will have to be coaxed with the promise of ducks and barges further up. But for now she can push him past mute and big eyed, chewing his dummy, placid, taking it all in. She doesn't think the noise affects him.

When she goes to his cot he's already awake and beams up at her, a spaceman fallen from the moon, spreadeagled, hugely pleased with himself. They curl up together on the sofa for his bottle, and she strokes his neck and his head, runs her finger along the place where the worst scar is almost healed, so much quicker than her own skin. She still has to plaster her neck with foundation, or wear boring high-cut T-shirts. Then she sees the time, stuffs everything she can think of into the nappy bag, wraps him up and straps him in and they're off into the growl, the low roar, the sea of noise. It is easier, almost exhilarating, to go out and face it, to take it on.

They cross the old railway bridge that spans a long thin field with apple trees and brown-and-white Gypsy horses. The horses are nervy, gallop around under the bridge as they go over; the noise must get to them too, she thinks. Past the docks where a huge metal scoop is lifting up water in its jaws and releasing it to smash down onto the concrete quayside. Bundled against the spring wind the baby rocks back and forth in his buggy as if riding a horse; if she could hear him he'd be crowing with delight. She laughs, pushes on up the hill. And then they are out of the noise, it is behind them, and they move into a different world. Past the workingmen's club, down through the marina. She points out ducks, bright-painted narrow boats, and wonders what it must be like to live like that. Not with a baby. Impossible. Imagine a toddler. And then on up the canal, about half a mile, always a bit further than she remembers. Not great shoes for walking but they were cheap and pretty and they make her feet look small. The pram isn't great either, her wrists and fingers tingle unpleasantly with the vibrations from the tarmac. Sometimes she passes families, at weekends usually, or during the holidays: smiling dads pushing those big three-wheelers with the fat tyres. Her sister got hold of one — a pram, not a bloke — and said it made all the difference.

The baby points at a duck with a hairdo like Elvis, floating along serenely. Duck, she says. Quack-a-duck. A boat chugs past and Elvis vanishes; the baby points at the boat. She loves this, she loves it so much: this thin strip of land between the canal and the wide shining Severn, just enough for a towpath and some scrubby trees, and, further up, mudflats broken up by the dark shapes of abandoned boats, a narrow field with cows and thistles. It has been spotting rain but the sun comes out for her now, everything glistens, and they reach the row of houses near the lock.

Hers is the one in the middle. She parks the muddy pram outside the front door and goes in to the kitchen to get herself a cup of coffee, making it stronger and sweeter than she really likes because she can feel the fatigue waiting to floor her and she has to keep going. Two and a half hours of cleaning, two if she's lucky, then back to get the baby at least ready for bed before Alison comes to have dinner and explain about the working-from-home scheme, selling beauty products. She's got that nice chicken for two in the freezer, and a bottle of wine, and it will be great if he sleeps, if he stays down. She sits on the doorstep in the watery sun. Last night, for the third time this week, she had to walk him up and down until she wept with exhaustion, and in the end had left him in his cot, like the social worker had said to do if nothing else worked: safe, warm, dry, full, dosed with Calpol, and still screaming. She had closed the door of their room and eventually fallen asleep on the sofa, curled up in pain against the noise which went through her like glass. The dreams she had then were worse than waking. They had taken him away as she always knew they would, as they took Lisa's baby away. Lisa's face crying; them both crying together, walking down the street; Stuart waiting for her at the Gloucester house. To wake then, about five in the morning, on her own sofa in her own place, and to realise yet again that they had taken Stuart and not her baby, was like bursting out of a smoke-filled room into fresh clean air.

She checks his straps and positions the buggy so that he can see the boats and the trees and the glinting of light on water, so that he can greet dog-walkers and passing prams. And though he would rather be in the house with her, crawling and dribbling on hoovered carpets, chewing the doormat, pulling open doors for crockery and detergents and climbing the stairs, he can at least see her coming and going between the rooms. She takes a breath and gets going.

Ten minutes later she is cleaning the downstairs toilet and he has had enough of the trees and the light; there have been no boats, no passers-by. He grumbles for a while, then gets louder, rocking backwards and forwards at an angrier gallop than before. She peels off pink gloves, snagging the nail again, and goes out to rummage for a shiny wrapped biscuit. He lights up with pleasure at the sight of it, and she leaves him, intensely focused, smearing his face with chocolate. The biscuit buys her just under fifteen minutes, and she has moved on to the kitchen when he starts up again, grubby and furious, straining to be out. This time she gives him a beaker of something sweet, gaining ten more minutes till he drops it. She picks it up for him. Three minutes. She lets him yell this time while she finishes the fridge, then goes to the front door again, sniffs him, hauls him out of the pram and to his utter delight changes him on the lino in the dining room. He kicks and crows, triumphant, grabbing at her hair with sticky loving fingers and then peeing everywhere for good measure. She hasn't got a full change of clothes in the bag, and, having cleaned him up a bit, has to put him back in the damp vest. He rolls out of her grasp and sets off with great optimism across the floor. The struggle to get him back in the pram is brutal, and after a few minutes they are both crying with frustration. She prays that no one will walk past, forces him into the harness, and then, to calm them both, pushes the pram a hundred yards up to the lock and back, hoping he will go off to sleep.

He doesn't want to sleep, but, on their return to the house, settles for another chocolate biscuit, and enjoys the noise of the hoover for a while. She works fast, tense, with an eye on the clock. There may not be enough time. When she thinks she has done a reasonable job on the downstairs rooms she lugs the hoover up to the bedrooms. As soon as she is out of range he starts to scream again. He is grubbier than ever and now, as she is only too aware, probably wet and uncomfortable too: she feels the cold raw patch against his skin as if it were her own. Without quite realising it she finds herself back downstairs, on the doorstep, looking at him helplessly: he is not in pain, he is upset and angry, and she has to keep cleaning. She kisses his wet face and goes back upstairs. It will be over soon, she tells him in her head, now don't cry, please don't cry, please don't cry. But the work is twice as difficult. She has to hoover everything again; the beds look rumpled; she knocks a waste bin over, begins to sob to herself: don't cry, please don't cry. She wants someone else to be responsible, even for a few hours. She is nineteen. She is tired.

The last bedroom is her favourite. Even now, standing hopelessly in front of the full length mirror, with her red nose and pale blotched skin and the tears and chocolate smeared all over her thin exhausted face; even now, with the knife-edge of his crying physically hurting her somewhere just under the ribs, she can feel the light coming off the water on both sides of her: a narrow room, like a boat, its windows looking out onto the canal in front and the river behind. A large double bed fits snugly under the eaves. What it must be like to sleep there, and to wake up with the quiet shining water on either side. Why do the owners live in Spain? she thinks again. When you could have all this. She plugs in the hoover and drowns out his noise, willing herself back together to finish the task, obliterating self-pity. And when she finally stops the machine's awful racket she hears a difference; he is calming down, going to sleep. He has found his dummy and is chewing it, and the familiar little moaning sounds are a blissful relief.

Just the bed. Calmly now, and methodically, she strips the duvet, the sheet, the pillowcases, and bags them up for the laundrette. Then she makes it all up again, in a soft bluey-grey cotton, her favourite of the three options rotated week on week. It looks beautiful. She goes to wipe over the little basin in the far corner, and, seeing herself in the mirror, washes her face in cold water. Clean now, and calm, and quiet at last. This beautiful room. What it must be like.

Only for a second, a minute, then, to imagine herself

waking up in this room like a boat between the river and the canal. She lies full length on top of the silvery blue duvet, closes her eyes and opens them, sees the way light reflects in the two mirrors and on the white sloping ceiling. Watches it flicker. Breathes in the quiet. Closes her eyes. And in the dreams that come then there are no raised voices, no faces and no fear, only a long peaceful sequence of events and places through which she walks with a sense of calmness, and the rhythm of her walking is like a baby breathing in his sleep.

When she opens her eyes, confused, she takes a long moment to remember where she is. All the colour has leeched away, something fundamental has shifted: the room is almost dark. And even then she is so muddled with sleep that it takes another long moment to work out what she can hear and why it frightens her. It is not the soft thrumming of heavy rain on the eaves above her head. It is the quiet.

Crossing

Of course it was gradual, like all these things — we'd notice it from visit to visit, a bit more, or rather less, each time. But you couldn't really say when it started. It's a process, I suppose, isn't it? An encroachment; the tide coming in.

And on to the next person, a cousin. Making sure she had a refill in my mother's blue china. Making sure the sandwiches went round, and around again, like my mother's conversation, oh a long time before the end.

But in the car on the way home my father said, You're wrong. I checked Robbie in the rear view mirror, but he was absorbed in his *Dr Who* cards. What about?

About not being able to say when.

When what?

When it started. You know — when she started.

Mum?

Yes.

Started?

Started not being there.

Oh.

I wasn't quite sure what he meant. I waited a bit, for him to go on, but he seemed to think he'd made his point. When I tried the subject again he just shrugged.

He stayed about three weeks, and there we were, three generations of males in the one house: Robbie off to school every morning, me off to work, and my father, usefully enough, pottering around the house and garden, tidying up, cooking for us most nights, weeding, mowing the lawn. We got along very well, which is more than many of my friends could claim about relationships with their own fathers. My mother moved in and out of our conversations naturally enough, as did Sophie. Presences around the place they were, in photos, of course, but also in things like cups and cushions, vases, books. My father seemed comfortable, and not excessively struck by grief. Robbie and I had our usual games, our walks, our inane conversations. I wondered if we should make the arrangement permanent.

Before I got round to asking him, a couple of things happened. There was an odd moment one Friday night, when we were down at the fish and chip place celebrating a home win for Robbie's team, and I was saying that we ought to be feeling guilty about eating cod with the stocks so low and why didn't you see haddock more often, it was supposed to be in better shape, and had more taste to it anyway, and Dad said he had no time for haddock and anyway wasn't it the batter we came for, and Robbie said no, it was the chips. And then: think of poor Granny having to eat limpets. I'd not heard this one before and was much intrigued. When did she eat limpets? I said, raising an eyebrow at my father. Oh, said Robbie vaguely, with the children — you know, she made the children go and collect them off the rocks at low tide. And I would have said, which children? only my father's face had frozen as if in pain. I thought he'd had an attack of some kind and got up in a hurry, scattering cutlery, but he shook off whatever it was almost immediately and reached for his tea. I sat down again and Robbie dived under the table for my fork.

And then I did it again. I did the whole saccharine set piece about the gradual encroachment of whatever form of mental deterioration it was that took my mother away when some friends came for dinner. We were sitting over coffee afterwards, relaxed — they were close friends — and for some reason their few quiet words of sympathy set me off: a quick sketch of her gradual decline, her slow drifting away from us, and so on, and it was only when my father got up abruptly to fetch some sugar for his tea that I realised with a little inward shock that I was repeating myself (repeating myself, for heaven's sake!) and had upset him in much the same way as before.

After they'd gone I fished a clean tea-towel from the drawer and went to help him with the washing up. He said he'd liked my friends, especially her. Good sense of humour. Nice evening altogether. And I said, nervous: I'm sorry if I said something stupid again, Dad. I think it's partly because I don't understand.

You don't, he said simply, and I thought I'd drawn another blank. But after he'd made his Ovaltine and I'd got myself another glass of wine we went back to the fire and he began talking. Do you remember a holiday in Scotland when you were about Robbie's age? He cast about for things that might have signified to a seven year old. A white horse in the field by the house. You got mauled by a bramble. Easter egg hunt on the beach.

Yes, dimly. A little black dog?

Yes. Belonged to the owners of the cottage. You were great friends.

Dad, that was forty years ago. You're not going to tell me that Mum's Alzheimers or whatever it was..?

Not that, no. But what happened became part of it.

There was an island, he said; it was just opposite the cottage, which was practically on the beach, a lovely little place. The island was tidal, and you could walk out to it and back during about four hours in the day, the times shifting. You and I went over once quickly near the beginning of the week, and I explored it for myself one morning while you lot were still asleep. It was special, I mean, she was right about that. Tiny scrap of an island, with everything you could possibly want: the ruins of a medieval chapel, a prehistoric barrow, a copse of fir trees, a couple of pocket-sized beaches, gorse and black-thorn at the back of the island growing almost flat against the rocks because of the wind; seals. I startled a deer that morning. And the house. Tucked in behind privet and flowering red-currant and forsythia growing untrimmed. It was white, a good size, built in the Twenties perhaps, with a walled garden; locked and boarded but you could easily imagine it being opened and aired when the family eventually came back or the heir was found. A sleeping beauty.

I fetched another glass of wine, feeling he'd taken something of a detour. And Mum?

End of the week. We took a picnic over at lunchtime, and that was her first visit. It had an effect on her. She was all sparkly, like a girl. I thought you might remember: we played hide and seek and she spent ages skimming stones with you in the cove.

It didn't sound quite like my mother, whose usual attitude to picnics was less carefree, more campaign-driven. But for a brief moment I could see us, or was it Sophie with the boy, poised for a throw and laughing at the water's edge.

A happy day, said my father with great determination. It was a happy day.

But?

We got back before the tide covered the bar, about six I suppose. Supper, bath and bedtime for you. You used to go —

I know, earlier than Robbie gets away with. It was a rare point of friction.

Hm. And the next day was our last. Your mother and I had some supper by the fire and I was looking at the brochures, thinking what we might do. I suggested a couple of things — steam trains was one of them — but she wasn't really listening, she was sitting there with her face all screwed up in concentration, looking at the tide tables. And when I asked her straight what she wanted to do tomorrow she looked up — it was almost apologetic, how she looked. And she said that what she most wanted was to spend a whole day on the island — to go early and be cut off by the tide, and then be liberated at low tide in the evening.

What a lovely idea. And did we?

Alone.

Alone?

She wanted to do it alone.

He got up stiffly, with a little shrug, and went off to the

toilet, leaving the full strangeness of this to settle on me. My mother was not a romantic, and hardly even one for the great outdoors. She was what they called in the Fifties a Home-Maker. Busy, gregarious, funny, no-nonsense, a good neighbour and, I still think it now, selfless in her absorption to the needs of her family. Which is not to say that she couldn't get cross or frustrated with us, but we, her child and her husband, I'm sure that we defined her. And we were close, loyal, the three of us. Ten years on from this one I remember being eaten away with guilt after I missed a family holiday to go to France cycling with a friend. To sabotage the last day of our week with an act of such reckless eccentricity was, quite simply, not something my mother could have done. And besides, I'd have remembered.

You had a row? I hazarded.

He sat back down, looking at me blankly. Why? No of course not, not like that anyway. I was upset, of course. Tried to talk her out of it. Worried what to tell you. But no. She went first thing, in the half-dark. You and I did the steam trains. I said she had a headache; then that she gone to the chemists, and, in the evening, for walk to clear her head. You had a new train by then. I don't think you were upset.

Who knows? I said sadly. Who knows what they think?

He looked at me gently. That lad's OK, he said. You're doing a grand job.

This craze — no, that's unfair — this enthusiasm for family history that has swept the land these last few years has made all kinds of skeletons rattle and dance. In my own circle of friends and colleagues alone I can think of several cases like mine where a revelation has had the effect of opening a door in a familiar house to find a new room with people in it who have been living there quietly unapprehended all along. One friend discovered a complete set of first cousins in New Zealand; another found out that her mother had had a previous marriage and family, completely erased from official history. But these lost people can be found. They exist in censuses, snapshots, graveyards; in phone directories and on the internet. On Saturday afternoons public libraries hum with the suppressed excitement of people chasing people, casting out lines to pull them in from oblivion.

But I, not far off fifty, having lost my real wife and my real mother, uncovered a clutch of purely imaginary brothers and sisters who made no mark of any kind on official records. Their very existence could only be inferred from scraps of knowledge given me by my seven-year-old son and my stubborn and still-wounded father; though I tried hard to remember things for myself, hints or phrases I ignored or didn't understand at the time, I couldn't help feeling that she hadn't wanted to tell me. Or have I just forgotten? And where the people in libraries sift doggedly through census returns I had to fish patiently for tiny details in conversations, mostly with Robbie. After that evening my father would not talk about the island, and soon afterwards he said he was ready to try living at home again. Robbie and I took him over at half term, and stayed a couple of nights. We did all the usual things: the park and the boating lake, the funny little zoo. Then we left him, busy in his neglected garden, and headed off for a few days by ourselves.

My first impulse was to hit the M6 and keep going, but I restrained myself, and was rewarded for it. We took a couple of days driving up, stopping at a vast indoor aquarium, where turtles and sharks swam improbably through perspex over our heads. A shoal of mackerel, wheeling like starlings, prompted a comment from Robbie about when Grandad was a fisherman. My father had been a bus driver, and then a lecturer in politics at a further education college, and I knew for a fact that he didn't even like fly-fishing. At an ostrich farm in the Eden Valley we stood watching the big pale eggs stubbornly not hatching in an incubator, and Robbie remembered how one of the girls — Sally, I think it was — had stolen half a dozen eggs from the kitchen and tried to hatch them in a pile of jumpers at the bottom of the wardrobe. How they stank. He'd got this story, he said, when he and Granny were making a cake together; which, I thought, had to have been at least a year or eighteen months earlier. When you were five or six. And how, in any case, can I reliably accept the things you tell me happened to you, you who still believe in dinosaur parks and the Easter bunny? But I couldn't stop fishing for bits of this phoney past.

There were four children, I decided, three girls and a boy. I never did work out if he — Jack — was me, or in addition to me, or if he somehow cancelled me out. (Presumably my father felt much the same about the fisherman.) And the girls? Wishes? Miscarriages? I had never even wondered, and could not now think how to ask, why I was an only child. But there they all were, an old-fashioned, happy-go-lucky sort of family, with a life a good bit rougher and more out of doors than mine had been in our quiet suburb. I suspected them of being plagiaries of the vigorous story-children of my youth: bright resourceful girls in torn pinafores getting into scrapes, with a little brother traipsing after them, teased and adored. In fact I had no idea how Jack fitted in with rest: he may have been the bossy eldest. History, or fiction, or psychosis, does not relate. And all of them busy in my mother's head as she washed up, mended, cleaned and cooked for us. If only she had written them down, I thought, it would have been less strange.

But she wrote nothing except lists and cards, and very occasionally letters on small sheets of pale blue notepaper.

The B&B was about a mile further up the coast, and after we had unpacked and amused ourselves with the packets of coffee and hot chocolate and the complimentary custard creams we set off along a path banked with bracken and creamy hawthorn and yellow gorse. Late afternoon, and the clouds had broken up enough for the sea to start shining as I had hoped it would. I smoothed the little wooden box in my pocket with the fingerful of ashes pilfered from my mother's urn (the rest had been scattered decently among the primroses in the memorial garden). When Robbie wasn't looking I would let them go quietly somewhere near the house, a gentle nod to a life not lived there, and that, I hoped, would be an end. No need to make a fuss about it with the boy; it would only confirm his muddled apprehension of my mother's past. Not that I was planning on setting him straight there either, plenty of time for the authorised version later. I'd brought a map, but I think I would have known we were nearly there without it. Although I'd planned the trip carefully in many respects I had left the tide to look after itself, and had no idea if we would be able to cross to the island at once, or would have to wait till tomorrow.

The causeway curved out to the island, almost black in the light of the shallow sea. We should wait ten minutes, I told Robbie, it's easy enough to see if the tide is coming or going: put a marker at the edge there. He ran ahead with a stick and I followed him over the beach. It was all boulders, small and egg-shaped, dark grey, and as I bent to pick one up I had the strangest feeling, a bolt of recognition, a memory locked into the stone, now triggered at the sight of a line of quartz that circled many of them like a thin white belt. It caught me like a blow on the chest. I wanted to sit down and weep, but I just stood there hopelessly as Robbie ran on ahead, and I saw in the evening light the bewitched woman making her way carefully, awkwardly back over the stones to the anxious man waiting and the boy playing nearby. They do not really come back, I thought. They do not ever really come back.